W9-CYE-383

Read and Rhyme LEVEL 1 ★

Pine to Swine

by Pearl Markovics

Consultant:
Beth Gambro
Reading Specialist
Yorkville, Illinois

Contents

BEARPORT PUBLISHING

New York, New York

Pine to Swine

I see a tall **pine**.

I see a long **spine**.

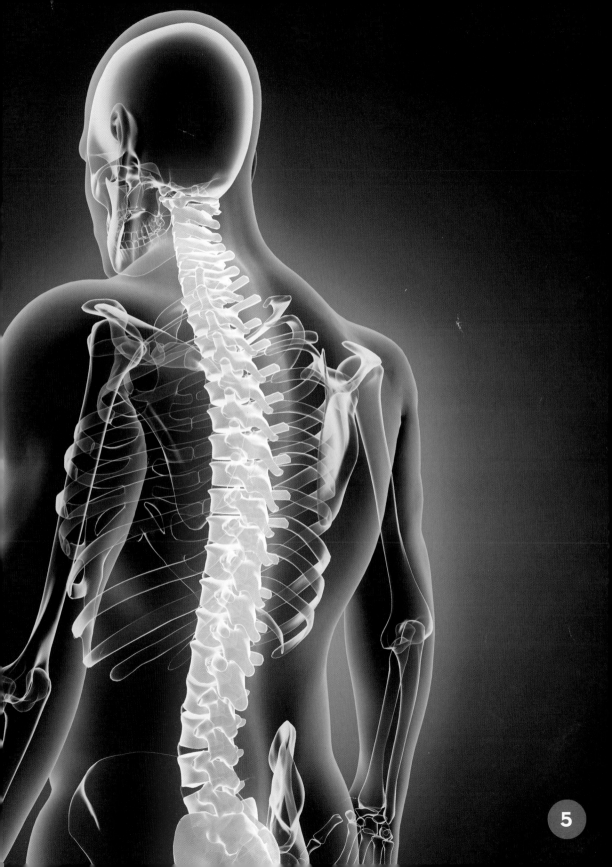

I see a
number **nine**.

I see a green **vine**.

9

I see a zigzag **line**.

I see red **twine**.

I see a big **swine**.

Key Words in the -ine Family

line

nine

pine

spine

swine

twine

vine

Other **-ine** Words: **dine, shine, whine**

Index

About the Author

Pearl Markovics enjoys having fun with words. She especially likes witty wordplay.